GENES

The Story of an Accidental Superhero

Dianne Bramble

ISBN

Cover illustration by Liam Bramble

Cover design by Liam Bramble

Foreword by Anna Bramble

About the Author by Tim Bramble

Printed and bound in Canada

This story is for all people around the world with Parkinson's Disease.

You are all heroes.

FOREWORD

My mother was diagnosed with Parkinson's Disease in 2013. I was almost 12 at the time. At this point, I had absolutely no idea what Parkinson's was, and I was convinced that everything was terrible and my mum was going to die (that is most definitely not what happens with Parkinson's, but if you mention anything with the word "disease" in it to a twelve year old, they might jump to conclusions). I soon learned that I overreacted and there was, in fact, not much to worry about, because now we knew what was making my mum so tired, and she could get proper treatment for it. Plus, my mum took it pretty well, so I really didn't think of it as much of a big deal. When it came up in conversation though, an astounding amount of people said stuff like "Oh no! That's awful, I'm so sorry!" as if someone had died. This confused me greatly, because like I said, my mum was quite alright. However, once my friends saw how my mum was doing, they understood why we weren't making a big deal about it. Several of my friends have said that my mother inspires them, and a few have even said that she is a "badass". I personally agree with them. No bias here. Anyway, from my perspective, not that much has changed for me, because my mum has things under control. Except misplacing her medications and constantly asking us (my brother and me) to go get them from various locations around the house/car. All things aside, my mother has been a fantastic role model to my brother and me, and I'm really proud of her for dealing with her diagnosis the way she did.

I think it's over. There haven't been any changes in three days and I'm feeling better than I've ever felt in my life.

Now what?

There are only a few people I can tell and I don't know how I'm going to hide what's happened to me. If people find out, I'll probably end up in a lab somewhere. Or worse.

I won't let that happen.

CHAPTER ONE

I started noticing problems when I was about 35 years old. First there was the fatigue, the mind numbing, overwhelming fatigue. I ignored it and wrote it off as being the mother of two children under the age of five. I felt exhausted every day and marvelled at all the things other women I knew seemed to be able to do. I doubted myself and eventually thought that I was less of a mother/wife/friend because I couldn't keep up with them. It was all I could do to push my way through the tiredness every day. People tried to be helpful by suggesting things like making lists, eating healthy, exercising and getting more sleep. I tried them all. Nothing worked, so I carried on as best I could.

But it was more than just fatigue. I had trouble sleeping and a strange jumpy feeling in my right arm and leg. It was harder to brush my teeth and stir things. I sometimes tripped over my right foot. I developed a frozen right shoulder and a small tremor started in my right pinky finger. My running, which had been going so well, started to backslide as my times got slower and slower. The flowers in my front garden didn't seem to have the same intense scent they used to have.

Taken separately, it was easy to explain away all these symptoms. Trouble sleeping: young kids. Jumpy feeling in my arm and leg: stress. Having a harder time brushing my teeth and stirring things: exercise more. Tripping over my own foot: pay more attention. Frozen shoulder: just needs time. Tremor in my pinky finger: fatigue. Poor running times: I'm over 35. Bland flowers: old bulbs. I had explanations for everything.

Eventually, I couldn't ignore the symptoms anymore. My family doctor was as perplexed as me. She sent me to several specialists. An internal medicine specialist attributed many of my symptoms to low iron. I was tested for Lyme disease, which was negative. My family doctor finally sent me to a neurologist.

Here's where my journey really begins.

I will never forget sitting in the neurologist's office after a long day of physical exams, interviews and waiting. I knew that something was up by the way he was acting. My husband was with me, thankfully. I wouldn't have handled the news the same way if he hadn't been there.

"You have Parkinson's." The doctor looked at me and told me that I have hemi-Parkinsonism to be exact, as it only affects the right side of my body. I started to cry. I don't really remember much of what was said after that. My mother's father had Parkinson's and even though I was pretty young when he died, I remember him as a man who could barely move or smile. He needed help with everything. All I could think about was how I didn't want to end up like that.

Parkinson's is a neurodegenerative disease - it has no cure and gradually gets worse. Movement is normally controlled by dopamine, a chemical that carries signals between the nerves in the brain. When cells that normally produce dopamine die, the symptoms of Parkinson's appear. By the time symptoms appear, about half the dopamine producing cells in the brain are already dead. There is no cure, only treatment and medications.

"Great," I thought, "my brain cells are killing themselves!" Lucky me. Parkinson's runs in my family, which is probably why I have it. It would be cooler if the Force was strong in my family, but no such luck! My neurologist (I never thought I'd say those words!) gave me a prescription, one of several that were to come, and off I went.

I spent the next few days crying a lot, telling my family and friends and trying to figure out how to tell my employers and coworkers. I was feeling pretty sorry for myself. Only a few months before my diagnosis, I had started a new job at a local physicians' office as a nurse. I was in a position where I was working directly with patients and their families to help them live with chronic conditions (I know - what a coincidence!). It was honestly the best job I'd ever had and I was terrified that I'd lose it.

So many things ran through my mind. Would people treat me differently or stop talking to me all together? Would I be able to keep working? What if I passed this disease to my kids? Would I still be able to travel? What did the future hold for me? I was a bit of a mess for awhile.

As time went on, things settled down. I took my medications, I exercised and tried to live a healthy lifestyle. With a few accomodations, I was able to continue working. I was not going to let this disease ruin my life!

And I was not going to give up on my dreams. I read about new developments in treatments and medications. Every time I saw my neurologist, we would discuss the newest research. He was very upbeat and encouraging about my future.

The treatment he was most excited about was gene therapy. I read a little about it, but it wasn't until I got a call from his office asking if I wanted to participate in a research study that I really considered it as an option. " Count me in!", I said.

CHAPTER TWO

Gene Therapy. I hadn't been involved in any Parkinson's research so far and this seemed like an amazing opportunity. This could improve my quality of life immensely. It may even be a cure! As I understood it, gene therapy was an experimental surgical technique that inserted healthy genes into a patient's own cells to treat a disease. Since it was experimental, it was only being used on people who had diseases with no known cure.

Not scary at all! I brought home all the paperwork and prepared to talk my husband into agreeing with the procedure. In a nutshell, I would have two small holes drilled into my skull. The surgeon would inject dead virus cells that had been injected with healthy DNA into the region of my brain that controls movement. No problem, right?!

My husband and I talked about the procedure for days, or was it a lifetime?! Part of me wanted to scream and tell him that I was going to do it with or without his blessing. It was *my* body and even though he is amazingly supportive, he will never know what it's like to have Parkinson's. I wouldn't wish it on anyone. It took a while to convince him, but he finally agreed that this would be an amazing opportunity. We signed the forms, sent them to the clinic and waited.

And waited. It was so hard not to think about it. Everytime the phone rang or I got an email or text my heart jumped into my throat. When it wasn't the clinic, there would be a moment of disappointment and then the waiting would start all over.

Finally, two weeks after signing the forms, I got a call asking me to come in for blood work and other tests to make sure I was a good candidate for the procedure. After being poked and prodded for what seemed like hours, I was home. Two agonizing days later, the results came back showing everything was a go and I was booked for the procedure the following week.

This was really happening. I was excited, scared, emotional, anxious and hopeful all at the same time. I told my parents and sister. I told my in-laws. I told all my friends and my coworkers. They were all happy for me, but worried at the same time. This could change my life forever. If the procedure went badly, I could be worse off or dead. If it didn't work, then I would be the same and move on to the next treatment. If it worked, there would be no more pain, stiffness, tremors, fatigue and slowness. I would be whole again. No one but another person with Parkinson's could really understand what this meant to me. This could be the answer for all of us.

CHAPTER THREE

Surgery day arrived. Did I already say that I've never been so excited, nervous and scared in my whole life? There was no way to prepare for a life-changing day like this. I didn't know what to expect or how to feel, so I went into it thinking, "What's the worst that could happen?".

I kissed my kids goodbye. I hoped they couldn't tell how scared I was as I told them I'd see them in a few days and I loved them. They looked worried and there were tears. I didn't want to leave them like that, but if I stayed much longer, I'd start crying too.

My parents had come up to help out with the kids and I gave them big hugs and told them I loved them too. My mom was trying hard not to cry and a single tear slid down my dad's cheek. It took all the strength I had not to cry. I put on a big smile, grabbed my husband's hand and walked out the door. He didn't say anything, but he returned the squeeze of my hand. He has no idea how much I love him.

The ride to the hospital was quiet and we walked in together still holding hands. The nurses were great. I was checked in and prepped for surgery in less than an hour. Finally, it was time. Before they wheeled me to the operating room, my husband leaned over and told me he'd see me after the procedure. We locked eyes and in that moment I knew that everything would be alright.

The operating room was stark. The doctors and nurses were just eyes and disembodied voices. Strapped to a table set almost to vertical with my head in a vice, I was relieved when they injected the medication to relax me. "We're ready to begin," I heard from one of the faceless doctors. The sound of the drill that was to bore two holes into my skull was petrifying, but at least there was no pain. So far, so good.

"Everything is going well. We're ready for the injections." Luckily, the brain can't feel anything and I couldn't see what was happening, so I didn't have to watch the needle going into my head. Just as the surgeon was performing the procedure, I thought I saw the lights flicker and I felt a bit of a shock, like you get from a static charge. No one said anything, so I assumed it was the drugs. A couple of injections and a few stitches later, I was in the recovery room.

So many doctors and nurses came to check up on me, I felt like a celebrity. My husband held my hand so tightly and looked so relieved, I could tell the waiting had been hard for him. Well, it's not over yet. Now we wait and see if the procedure was a success.

Day one post-op, I felt pretty good. I had a slight headache (probably from the two holes in my head!), but I was able to get up and walk around. My Parkinson's symptoms improved slightly, so the doctor reduced my medications. He assured me he hadn't seen such a quick change in other patients. He was very optimistic.

 "With any luck, you'll be able to stop taking some of your medications all together." Music to my ears!

Day two post-op I was released from the hospital. My parents, kids, sister, in-laws, niece and nephews were all waiting for me at home. Meals were made, the house was cleaned and I was pampered for about a week and then everyone went home and things returned to normal - or so I thought.

Day 8 post-op I had my first follow-up appointment with the surgery team. My symptoms had improved so much that I had reduced my medications to the point that I was on the lowest doses possible. I was moving with almost no rigidity, my tremor was almost completely gone and best of all, I felt more energetic.

My neurologist confirmed that I was doing very well, better than any of the other research participants so far, and he took me off all my Parkinson's medications.

"Don't get too excited," he warned. "This is still early stages of the study. We don't know whether you will continue to improve, stabilize here, or even regress."

I didn't care. For the first time in a long time, I felt normal, and I was going to hold onto that feeling as long as I could.

Day 13 post-op, I began to notice further changes. My running speed was improving to a point where I was faster than I had ever been. Before I experienced Parkinson's symptoms, my best 5km race was 27 min, and that time increased every year as the disease progressed. At one point I was running a 39 min 5km race. I had been given the all clear to resume physical activities, so I started running and meeting with my personal trainer again. My new best 5km time was 22 min and I wasn't even breathing hard at the end.

The fatigue was gone and I didn't need as much sleep. In fact, I was averaging 5-6 hours of sleep a night and still felt energetic. I no longer needed naps during the day, even on my busiest days.

I was getting physically stronger - my trainer even remarked that I was going to have to buy heavier weights soon! I couldn't believe how much better I was feeling.

Day 15 post-op I noticed that my sense of smell was returning. In fact, it was more sensitive than it had been pre-Parkinson's. Not always a benefit, but If that was the worst thing to happen to me, I would happily live with it.

I didn't think too much about these new "improvements" at first - it was exciting to see how much I had changed. Then things started to get a little weird. Other things started to improve - my vision was getting better (I had worn glasses for distance since I was 12), scars and wrinkles were starting to disappear, aching joints stopped hurting. Even my grey hair was disappearing.

I wondered if I should worry. Was this normal? Were the changes going to stop? If they didn't, what would happen to me? My husband noticed that something was bothering me, so I shared with him what had been happening.

"Call the neurologist. I don't remember him saying anything about this kind of thing as possible side effects," he urged.

Clearly, he was worried about me. I don't know why, but I convinced him that we should give it a couple of weeks and see what happened.

"Don't worry," I promised. "If things get out of control, I'll call the doctor right away."

But promises can't always be kept.

CHAPTER FOUR

This is crazy! Day 17 post op, and now I can't wear my glasses. I tested my vision at work and I could easily read the bottom line. I've started telling people that I'm wearing contacts. Since I no longer have grey hair or wrinkles, I've been telling people that I started dying my hair and using anti-aging creams. My hearing is almost too sensitive. I can hear people whispering in other rooms and I'm really not impressed with my sense of smell. I wasn't aware that there are so many horrible odours in the world. Now I have some idea of what dogs must go through.

My 5km run time is 15 mins and I don't even break a sweat. I can bench press my body weight easily and pull-ups are a breeze. I just don't seem to get tired.

I only sleep for about 2 hours a night and I'm rarely tired. I get so much done now! My house has never been so organized and clean. I've even painted the entire house and am making plans to build some raised gardens in the backyard.

 It's all fascinating and worrisome at the same time. I wish I had access to a lab and someone I can trust to tell me what's going on. In the movies, the hero always has a scientist who can help.

I'm starting to lie to my family, people at work, my trainer, my friends and my doctors. They wouldn't understand what's happening and it would just freak them out. It's better that they don't know.

Part of me is excited and can't wait to see how strong I become. The other part is scared. What if the changes don't stop? How strong could I get before I lose control? How much can my body take?

My husband is terrified, but I convinced him to keep my secret. I'm afraid that if I tell my doctors what's happening, they'll want to run all sorts of tests and I'll become a lab rat.

"'I'll give it two more weeks. If things continue to change, I'll go see my doctor," I promise myself." Maybe."

Day 30 post op and I was driving home from work thinking about the latest changes. I tested my vision at work again and I could read the bottom line from 60 feet away instead of the normal 20 feet. It feels like I could do anything at this point - maybe I could fly? I don't think I'll test that one.

My thoughts were interrupted by the sound of squealing tires, breaking glass, the crunch of metal and screams. Two cars had hit head-on on the country road ahead of me. I quickly called 911, reported the accident and our location and told them I was going to check on the cars' occupants since I was the only one around who could help.

The driver of the first car was dead. Inside the second car, there was a woman in the driver's seat and a small child in a car seat in the back. Neither was conscious, but I could hear them breathing. The smell of smoke was overpowering and I realised that the car was on fire. I tried opening the doors, but they were jammed shut from the impact. I panicked. I had to get them out. I pulled as hard as I could and the door ripped off. I managed to get the car seat unbuckled and carried the seat and child to a safe location. I ran back to the car, which was really burning now. I pulled the driver's seat belt so hard that it snapped. I grabbed the woman and carried her to where the child was. As I assessed their injuries, the firefighters and police arrived. I told them what I had witnessed and they quickly got to work putting the fire out, directing traffic and getting things under control. The paramedics showed up soon after and took over the care of the woman and her child. Once they were stable, they loaded them and took off with their sirens blaring.

I was still in shock when a police officer came over and started asking me questions. As I started recounting the series of events, I realised that there were some things I was going to have to get creative about. It was kind of good that the car had burned. It would be harder for the investigators to tell that I had ripped a door off and snapped a seatbelt in two. It was a little harder to explain how I carried a full-grown woman by myself 100 metres. After all, I'm only 5 feet 2 inches and 110 lbs soaking wet. I couldn't believe what I had just done - how would the police? I managed to blurt out a semi-coherent statement and hoped the officer would attribute my pauses and stumbles to shock. The officer seemed satisfied with my story and gave me her card, telling me that they may need to contact me if they had any more questions. I sure hope they don't. I'm not a very good liar.

I'm not sure how I got home and when I got there, I wasn't sure what to do. I felt a mixture of emotions - fear, sadness, exhilaration and excitement. The whole situation was the biggest rush I'd ever felt. I was a superhero! But where do I go from here?

CHAPTER FIVE

I think it's over. There haven't been any changes in three days and I'm feeling better than I've ever felt in my life.

Now what?

There are only a few people I can tell and I don't know how I'm going to hide what's happened to me. If people find out, I'll probably end up in a lab somewhere. Or worse.

I won't let that happen.

That sounds like the opening to a very cliche movie, but it's my life. It's been six months since I had the procedure and if If things stay the way they are, I will be like a superhero. I have abilities. This is so cool, a dream come true for a science fiction geek like me, but I have no idea how to handle this. Do I get a costume and go around town at night fighting crime? Do I hide my abilities and hope nobody finds out and they go away? Do I just try to live a normal life and only use my abilities in situations like the car accident? My brain hurts thinking about all the possibilities.

My husband and I spent days talking about what to do. He's the only one who knows. But we have so many questions, like can I still get hurt? Can I be killed? Will these abilities last? Am I obligated to help people? What if people find out what I can do? How do I hide what I can do? What if I hurt or kill someone by accident? If I try to help, will the police consider me a vigilante and try to arrest me?

This isn't like the comic books or the movies. I have a husband and 2 kids. I have parents, a sister, nephews and a niece, aunts and uncles, cousins, in-laws and friends. If I start to use my abilities to help people and I'm discovered, will that put all the people I care about and love in danger? If the wrong people find out, will I disappear and become a test subject? Is that even a thing?

How did this become my life? I just wanted to relieve my Parkinson's symptoms and now I'm a freak. My life just became more difficult than I can imagine.

After talking with my husband, I decided that I'd just try to live as normal a life as possible and see if the abilities remained. My husband was supportive, even though It couldn't have been easy for him to have a superhero for a wife.

Despite my best intentions, it was hard not to test how much I could do. At night, when everyone was sleeping, I'd go out and run. If I really pushed myself, I could run 5km in 8 mins. I ran 100m in 5 seconds - not exactly the Flash, but eat my dust Usain Bolt!

I could easily lift heavy objects around the house like the fridge - comes in handy when something rolls under there.

I was getting better at controlling my enhanced hearing and sense of smell. That is a huge relief - there are so many things I never wanted to hear or smell again!

As I was learning to live with and control my abilities, I made a mistake and tried to move the car out of my way in the garage. I slipped and cut my hand quite badly. Apparently I can still get hurt, which means I am most likely killable - good to know.

As I was cleaning the wound in the bathroom sink, I could see that it was already starting to heal.

"Ok, so I'm going to go with the idea that I can get hurt, but as long as the injury isn't too bad I'll recover very quickly," I thought to myself. But it's probably best to stay away from life threatening situations. I don't want to test whether or not I can heal from a mortal wound!

I was doing pretty well staying away from dangerous situations. That is until the other day. It was my day off and I was on Facebook when a post came up with a story about a missing child abducted in a nearby town while on his way home from school. The police thought the abductor was headed in my general direction in a gray van. I had to do something, so I got in my car and started driving around looking for suspicious vans. I used my 'super' hearing to listen for odd sounds and sure enough, as I passed a gray van, I heard what sounded like whimpering. I turned my car around and followed the van to a remote property off the main road. I called 911 and gave them an anonymous tip then parked my car far enough away that the police wouldn't see it and ran as fast as I could back to the laneway the van turned down.

Sure enough, there was a dingy old farmhouse. I could hear crying from inside the house, so I walked right up to the front door and knocked. What was I thinking! Everything went quiet inside and I started to panic. I tried opening the door but it was locked. I pulled it off the hinges and ran inside. My senses were overwhelmed by the stench in the house and the sound of the child crying. Before I could make a move towards the basement door where I could hear the child, a man appeared in the hallway holding a baseball bat.

"Get the hell out of my house!" he shouted and ran at me swinging the bat.

Adrenaline kicked in and cleared my senses. As he swung the bat at my head, I ripped it out of his hands and took him out at the knees. He went down fast, screaming and clutching his leg. How hard did I hit him?

I couldn't waste time thinking about it. The police would be there soon; I could hear the sirens. I pulled the door to the basement off its hinges and ran down to check on the little boy. I made sure he was alright and told him the bad man wouldn't hurt him and the police were almost there.

"Are you Wonder Woman?" he asked.

I told him no, but I knew her and he gave me a big smile. I smiled back and said that I had to go fight more crime and managed to get out of the house just before the police pulled up.

What a rush! I had to sit in my car for a few minutes to calm down. I wasn't sure if my feelings were good or not. I had saved a little boy from who knows what, but I had probably permanently disabled another human being. Granted, he wasn't a very nice human being, but he was still was a human being.

I scoured the internet and the news for any reports of the abducted boy. The only information I could find was that there had been an anonymous tip that had led the police to the boy. He was safe, unharmed and the suspect was in custody. There were no reports of anyone else being involved. The police must be wondering who called in the tip and injured the suspect. At least their only leads were coming from a little boy who believes in Wonder Woman and a child abductor.

"What have I done?' I thought.

If I continued to play superhero, I needed to ask myself some serious questions. On the lighter side - how would I get a costume and what would I call myself? On the more serious side - how far was I willing to go? Was I willing to kill someone? What if I couldn't and someone else died because of my inaction? What if I got caught and I went to jail, or worse? What if someone I hurt found out who I was and tried to hurt my family?

I was so confused and I needed someone to help me figure this out. My husband and I had already talked about this and I could tell he was scared for us and for me. I couldn't tell him about the guy at the farmhouse - he'd lose his mind!

The only other person I could think to talk to was my sister. We're really close and I knew she would listen. I was headed to the city where she lives for my daughter's track meet, so I called her and asked if we could meet at some point while I was there. She agreed and we set a date.

CHAPTER SIX

As soon as I arrived at my sister's, she knew something was up. As usual, she let me start the conversation and listened while I spilled my guts. I talked for what seemed like hours. When I got to the end of my story, she looked at me and said, "We can work through this together."

How did I get so lucky? Both my husband and my sister are the best people I know. If I didn't have them, I'm not sure how I would have handled this.

We spent several hours researching anything to do with genetic therapies, clinical trials and even conspiracy theories about genetic research. Although not particularly helpful, the material was at least entertaining.

Needless to say, we didn't learn very much. I was getting a little dejected until my sister said,

"Listen, I know a few people from a local think tank and they love "theoretical" problems like this. Let me talk to them and present this situation to them as brain teaser."

I'd love to be a fly on the wall during that conversation! I was promised a detailed account of their conclusion once they reached one. I left with a lighter heart knowing that I had another ally to help me deal with my situation.

On the long drive home, my daughter was unusually quiet. I asked her what was wrong, expecting her to say something like she was feeling like she could have done better in her track events, but her answer surprised me.

"Mom, I know you've been lying to me about something. You always said we could talk about anything, share anything. Why don't you trust me with whatever this is?"

I've never felt so horrible in my life. Ours was a relationship built on trust and I had disappointed her. I had a lot to make up for in the few hours we had left in the car.

I started by apologizing for not confiding in her. I hoped that after she heard what had been going on for the last few months, she'd understand and forgive me. Over the next few hours, I told her the whole story and explained that I didn't tell her earlier because I wanted her to be safe.

"You're quiet," I said. "Do you have any questions, cause I sure do!"

"Mom, what do you think your superhero name should be?"

We laughed so hard, I thought I would have to pull over. I've never been so relieved in my life. My daughter is the greatest. One thing she made me promise to do when we got home was to tell my son what was going on. I agreed that it was probably time.

We were having a really great conversation when all hell broke loose ahead of us. If my senses weren't as good as they are, we would have ended up in the pile of cars and trucks with everyone else. It took everything I had to guide the car off the highway to safety. Once we had stopped, I took a few deep breaths and then tried to make sense of the horrific scene. There were cars and trucks everywhere. I have no idea what caused the accident, but it looked like there were at least 20 vehicles involved. People were screaming and some of them had gotten out of their cars. The smell of fuel and blood was overwhelming to me. My senses were being overloaded. My daughter grabbed my hand and started talking to me in a calm voice. I focussed on her and managed to bring myself back to reality. As I looked at her, my thoughts started to coalesce and I told her to call 911 and stay in the car.

The scene was like nothing I'd ever witnessed and I truly hope I never see anything like it again. A few of the cars looked like scrap metal and I knew that anyone inside them had to have been killed instantly. I tried to focus on the people I could help by going vehicle to vehicle, searching for signs of life.

Other people had stopped to help and we started coordinating a search plan. We went in pairs, trying to match people with medical training with people who looked strong. I was matched up with an off duty firefighter and as we started our search.

I heard a woman calling for help. I started moving in the direction the voice came from and quickly realised the problem. The car the woman was in was jammed between two trucks. I couldn't believe that someone could still be alive in there. I looked at my partner and we made our way to the car. Sure enough, in the only space left in the mangled car was the woman. We assessed her and determined that her injuries were minor, but we needed to get her out of there. There was always the risk of fire and of more vehicles becoming involved. We began trying to pry any part of the car open, but it was so mangled that it was hard to pick a spot to work on. The woman was starting to panic, so I made a decision. I got up on the roof of the car, grabbed onto the only edge I could find and pulled as hard as I could. It began to give way and in a few seconds, I had opened up a space big enough to crawl through. She and the firefighter stared at me like they'd seen a ghost. I didn't know what to say, so I told them that we needed to get her to the paramedics and keep looking for more survivors.

The whole ordeal lasted for several hours. In all, ten people were dead and many more were injured. My partner and I had rescued twelve people and I had used my abilities at least three times. I really hoped that the injured would think that what they saw me do was related to adrenaline or that they had hit their heads and were hallucinating. I hadn't given anyone my name, so as soon as I could, I left the accident scene, got back in my car and continued the drive home.

As I told my daughter what had happened, I realised that I may have just made my life a lot more complicated. What if someone had taken my picture? What if the firefighter told the police, or worse, the media what I had done? He saw me do things a person twice my size couldn't have done, adrenaline or not. There's no going back now.

I called my husband to let him know what had happened and that we were alright. News of the accident was spreading fast and there were reports of a very strong woman who saved several people. Like in a game of telephone, the details had become distorted. The latest report had me at least six feet tall and looking like a bodybuilder. Maybe I got away with it?

Once we were home, I sat down with my son and told him everything. Then we sat down as a family and tried to come up with a way that we could deal with our new reality.

"Mom, this is the coolest thing ever! We have to think of a superhero name," my daughter gushed.

"And I can design the costume!" exclaimed my son.

My husband and I tried repeatedly to impress on them that this is not a comic book or a movie. This is real life and it could get real ugly.

"We have to keep this secret. From everyone, even your friends," we stated in no uncertain terms. "For our safety."

"Look, I can't promise I won't use my abilities again. If a situation arises and I can help, I don't think I would be able to just stand by. But I'll be more careful. I'll try to keep my face hidden…"

"So you do need a costume! At least a mask!" my son proclaimed.

What have I gotten myself into?

CHAPTER SEVEN

It's nearly nine months post-op and things are still okay. No government agents have broken down our door and taken me away. The police haven't tried to contact me and neither have the media. So far I have managed to dodge a few bullets, but I don't know if I can keep hiding in plain sight.

I actually went to a costume store and bought a mask. I felt like everyone was looking at me. A cheap purple halloween mask. This has got to be the worst superhero costume ever!

If I was actually going to continue to use my abilities, I would need a better disguise, but where does one get a kick-ass costume that's easy to carry around and put on in a hurry?

As I thought about what I could do for a costume, my daughter told me that I should get a black leather jacket to go with the mask. She also thought that I should keep a pair of leather gloves handy - I was probably leaving fingerprints all over the place. It's a good thing I'd never been arrested. At least there were no fingerprints on file.

I took my daughter's advice and bought a kick-ass black leather jacket. I also bought a very stylish leather backpack to carry my "costume". I felt like an idiot - what was I thinking?

I had a few more incidents over the next few months, but nothing as serious as the highway accident. That's a good thing. I wasn't sure I could handle that sort of thing very often. At least I don't sleep very much so I don't have a lot of time to dream. I wonder if superheros get PTSD?

My kids were having a great time trying to come up with a superhero name for me. I tried to discourage them, but they thought it was the best game ever. I have to admit that they were getting pretty creative.

"Purple Haze!"

"Lilac Defender!"

"Parkinson Power!"

"Purple Fox!"

And the list went on. It seemed that every day they came up with at least two or three more names.

My husband and I decided that we needed to have a talk with kids about discretion. We were afraid that they were getting too comfortable with my abilities and that they might say something by accident to their friends.

They were slightly offended that we were concerned about their ability to keep a secret.

"Mom, we get it! It's important, it's for our safety, blah blah blah!"

"Yeah! By the way we keep secrets from you all the time so I know we can… Wait… I mean, just trust us ok!"

They really are great kids. I couldn't ask for any better.

Now that we had settled into a new routine, I knew I needed to sit down with my husband to see how he was coping with everything. He talked for quite a while about his feelings and I did my best to listen and not interrupt. It was important that he had a chance to vent. His life had been turned upside down too.

At first he was reluctant to say much. I think he felt t guilty about complaining, but I convinced him that whatever he was feeling needed an outlet. He was feeling many things - fear that I would be discovered, fear that I would get hurt or killed, awe at what I could do, proud of the lives I had saved and jealous. He felt inadequate sometimes, even though he knew intellectually that he didn't need to feel that way.

I hadn't really thought about that. I was so busy trying to figure things out for myself, that I had forgotten he must be going through his own stuff. We resolved to talk to each other more often and to stop trying to protect each other.

Another issue we had to deal with was the fact that I had been avoiding my neurologist. I'd missed my last two check-ins and he was getting suspicious. In order to keep performing the procedure, he had to have accurate results from all his patients or the program could be cancelled. I didn't want that to happen because the vast majority of people who had the procedure found that their symptoms improved and their lives became much easier. I didn't want people to suffer because of me, but at the same time, I had to protect myself.

We tried to come up with ways I could fake being "super". I'm sure he'd believe that I was dying my hair, but how would I explain my lack of wrinkles and glasses? I could hide my strength and enhanced senses, but what would my blood work show? This was getting very complicated. We finally decided that I should book an appointment and trust that we could tell him everything.

The day of my appointment arrived and my husband and I waited nervously. The nurse called my name and we went into the office. She took my blood pressure and asked my the usual questions - how are your symptoms, any new issues, have I had to start taking any medications again, and so on.

The neurologist came in shortly after. He looked at me curiously and told me that I looked very well. He did the usual tests of balance, strength and mobility and sat back in his chair. He looked puzzled and said,

"I have to say, I've never seen a patient this well off after the procedure. In fact, you still seem to be improving. Nobody has had results like this so far in the study. I'd like to run some more tests. Blood work, CT scan and so on." .

I looked at him and told him that I would prefer not to have the additional testing and waited for his response. He, of course said that he needed the data for his research and to possibly help other patients improve. He noticed that I was nervous and tried to reassure me that the testing would be a breeze compared to the surgery. I told him I wasn't nervous about that, but I really didn't want any further testing. I looked at my husband and he nodded.

"You don't understand," I blurted out. "I'm not just improving, I'm… super!"

I told him about my abilities, leaving out the part about the costume and actually using my abilities several times, and waited to hear what he had to say.

He was quiet for what seemed a very long time. Then he laughed. I don't think he believed me, so I picked him up - chair and all. When I put him down, I thought he might pass out.

"OK, I think I understand why you don't want the testing. But, now I think it's even more important than ever that we figure out what's going on.".

He was confident that he could keep the results secret but he wanted to know what had happened and he needed to make sure that I was really okay. My husband agreed with him. I reluctantly followed suit.

CHAPTER EIGHT

The testing took almost two weeks to complete and my neurologist made sure that as few people as possible were involved. Other people (nurses, lab techs, xray techs) were given various reasons why the tests were being done.

We were nervous when we went back to his office to hear the results of the testing.

"Well, I can't find anything wrong with your test results," he said as he leaned back in his chair. "Your cells are regenerating at an incredible rate, but it doesn't seem to be causing any damage."

Despite that reassurance, he was concerned since he couldn't understand why I had reacted this way to the procedure and others hadn't.

He promised to keep my secret as long as I agreed to come in for testing every six months. I assured him that I would.

When we got home, our kids came running up to us with worried looks on their faces. They had been on YouTube and came across a video that had been posted a few months ago. The quality was pretty bad , but because it was a video taken at the scene of the highway accident, I was pretty sure what I was going to see. Sure enough, through the smoke, was the image of a small woman ripping the roof off a car! My heart sank and my mind started spinning. I didn't think anyone would recognise me from the video, but I was out there now. The video had over a million views and they had even given me a name - Amazon.

I read all 3000 comments . Most of them were what I expected - this is a hoax, there's no such thing as a superhero, this is staged, etc., but there were some (the ones who'd given me a name) who were really excited about the prospect of a real superhero. Their comments were more along the lines of - wow, who is she? is she an alien? where do you think she comes from? Some of these people even started writing stories about me.

Then there were the people who crawled out of the woodwork to call me things like demon, mutant, mistake, and called for not only my arrest, but my destruction. I guess I shouldn't be surprised. A certain segment of the population is always threatened by things they don't understand. What a mess!

The questions started all over again. My brain was racing and I couldn't turn it off. I made up scenario after scenario and none of them ended well. I either ended up in some government lab or dead. I didn't know how to deal with this, but I couldn't stop helping people if they were in trouble - could I? Could I be in a situation where people needed my help and not use my abilities? What if someone died and I could have saved them? Is saving myself more important than saving others? Was Gene Roddenberry right when he wrote the phrase "the needs of the many outweigh the needs of the few"? What would he think of my abilities? What would Stan Lee think? Maybe he'd have some advice. I need a vacation!

My husband tried to reassure me that everything would be okay, but I don't think he really believed that. I decided to do my best to stay optimistic. I mean, this isn't a comic book or a movie. There are no super-villains or evil aliens lurking around. I'm not going out of my way to find trouble. All I've done so far is help a few people. I can keep this under control, right?

CHAPTER NINE

I've started meditating. It's helping with the racing thoughts and I'm finding it easier to focus. It's getting easier to lie to people about the more obvious changes like my hair and lack of glasses.

I almost blew it the other day at work though. I was distracted thinking about a patient and tore my office door off the hinges. I tried to explain it by saying that I had noticed that the hinges were loose and I had forgotten to tell anyone. They really had no choice but to believe me - there was no other logical explanation.

I'm so used to my abilities now that I rarely think about it when I'm using them, especially at home. Like the incident at work however, this complacency has come close to exposing me more than once. Picking up heavy objects in stores, running to catch up to people who've dropped things, asking people if they've heard or smelled things they couldn't possibly have heard or smelled.

Sometimes I think I want people to find out about my abilities. I mean, it would be cool to have fans and be acknowledged for the things I've done, but at the same time, I really like my privacy.

Unfortunately, my desire for privacy may have come to an abrupt end. I am not proud of what happened next, but I can't change what I've done. I'll let you be the judge.

I was leaving work at the same time as a Muslim patient I recognized. We smiled at each other and made our way to our cars. That's when I heard three male voices approaching us from behind. They were shouting insults at the patient, telling her to go home and threatening her. I walked towards her and asked her to get in her car, lock the doors and call 911. She didn't hesitate.

When I turned around, I was shocked to see one of the men was holding a gun. What was he thinking?

"There are security cameras in the parking lot and lots of people watching. Are you sure you really want to do this?" I asked the man.

"My beefs not with you, but if you don't get out of the way, I'm not responsible for what happens to you! Those people need to go home before they get all of us killed!" he shouted.

"The police are on their way. There's still time to change your mind and end this before anyone gets hurt" I pleaded with him.

His eyes changed and I could tell that he'd made up his mind. He was going to shoot that woman. In a split second I charged him. The gun went off as I grabbed it and crushed it into an unrecognizable shape. I was so angry that I had to focus on my breathing to calm myself down. I took a quick glance back at the woman in the car to make sure she was okay. - Luckily, the shot had gone wild and hadn't injured anyone nearby.

The three men were staring at me like they'd seen the devil himself. The ringleader came at me. From somewhere in his clothing, he'd pulled out a rather large knife. How many weapons did this guy have? The people who'd been in the parking lot had retreated back into the clinic.

I only had a second to decide what to do. The police hadn't arrived yet, so I defended myself. He never stood a chance. By the time it was over, he had several broken bones, was unconscious and somehow I had broken his knife in half. The other two men started to run, but by that time the police had arrived.

How was I going to explain this? What were the witnesses going to say? I think what I did could land me in jail, at the very least for excessive force. I was defending myself and the other woman, but that didn't justify how badly I hurt the guy. I know there are people who would say he deserved it, but I lost control and now someone was very badly injured. I never thought I could be that person.

The doctors at the clinic made sure I hadn't been hurt and then the police took me down to the station to get my statement. I told them as much as I could without going into details about my abilities. They looked at me for a few seconds and asked me where I'd done my martial arts training. They said that several witnesses told them that I looked like a ninja. They couldn't understand how someone my size could do so much damage to a man twice my size. I actually did take jiu jitsu for a year when I was 16, so I embellished that story a little bit in the hopes that they would think it sounded somewhat plausible.

I asked about the guy I'd injured and they told me that he'd live. At least I hadn't killed anyone. As I waited for them to say I was free to go, one officer put the misshapen gun on the table, along with the broken knife. I told them that I honestly don't remember what happened to the knife. I guessed that it had broken during the struggle since I didn't have any cuts on my hands. Maybe one of us had stepped on it?

As for the gun, I stared at it and wracked my brain for a logical explanation as to how it ended up like that. I started to sweat and I know my heart started beating faster. There was no logical explanation. I started to stammer out a response saying that everything happened so fast that I really don't remember what happened.

"Maam, we have witnesses who say they saw you crush this gun with your bare hands. How do you explain that?" asked the officer.

I tried to look shocked.

"I certainly don't remember crushing the gun. Maybe my adrenaline levels spiked. I've heard stories of people lifting cars off when loved ones are in trouble. It must have been something like that," I responded.

They didn't look very convinced, but really, what were they going to say? They couldn't very well ask me if I was some kind of super woman!

I asked if I was being charged with anything. They said that since it was self-defense and I was trying to protect the other woman that they weren't going to press charges. They wanted me to be available though if they had any more questions. I agreed and went home to figure out what new trouble I had caused myself.

CHAPTER TEN

I realised after I got home that the police now had my fingerprints from the mangled gun and broken knife. Now I had to be more careful than ever. Sometimes I think it would be easier to just call the press and get the whole thing over with. At least then I wouldn't have to worry about being discovered. Maybe notoriety would offer me some protection from 'secret government labs' too!

The idea started to grow on me. I steeled myself for the talk with my husband going over all the arguments I could think of in my head. When he came home from work, I sat him down and started into my prepared speech. I gave him a few minutes to process what I had said and then asked him what he thought. He said he needed to think about it. Fair enough. If I went ahead with the idea, our lives would change yet again.

After a few hours of thinking and worrying, my husband told me he reluctantly agreed to go along with my plan, but he wanted us to tell our families and friends first. That sounded fair to me - I was thinking the same thing. We wanted to tell everyone in person, so we started arranging meetings.

We invited our parents, siblings and their families to our "20th anniversary party". We originally had been planning a small get together for our anniversary, so it wasn't too far of a stretch to get them to come up for the party. We held it at our house, so we could talk without worrying about being overheard. After dinner and dessert, we gathered everyone into the sunroom for coffee. They knew something was up and looked at us anxiously.

We talked for about an hour, back and forth with lots of questions from everyone. At the end of the evening, everyone was exhausted and we really weren't any closer to making a decision. There were lots of good points made; keeping my abilities secret was the safer route as long as I could keep myself out of trouble. It would also keep my family safer. On the other hand, if I went public then I wouldn't have to worry about being discovered.

One of the points made was that if I went public, people would try to get in touch with me all the time for help, kind of like winning the lottery. So many "friends" come out of the woodwork. Maybe I could do a lot of good though.

The only thing we could all agree on was to give it some time and really think about this decision. Whatever I decided, it would have a profound effect on my life and the lives of my family.

I wasn't in any hurry to make the decision. By nature, I'm very shy and I like my privacy. But despite my best intentions, it's been less than a year and already my family and neurologist know my secret. Would I really be able to keep the secret even if I tried?

The next hurdle was telling our friends.

Again, we planned a party. Our closest friends were invited and as the night arrived, the nerves started. I was pretty sure that things would be fine, but there's always a chance that things might go off the rails. When we told them about my original diagnosis, our friends were very supportive and never treated me differently. I couldn't ask for better friends.

We finished dinner and, again, moved to the sun room. We started the conversation and at first they were pretty sure we were joking. After they stopped laughing, I told them I could prove it and asked them what I could do to show them I wasn't pulling their legs.

Some of them got a funny look on their faces as they realised that I was serious. The joker in our group came up with the idea that I could bench press him. His wife looked at him like he was crazy. I agreed and we got set up. After I had pressed him ten times with no signs of tiring, I asked him if he'd had enough. Nobody said a word as I set him down.

This was weirder than when we told our families. I couldn't tell what they were thinking and I was getting very uncomfortable. One of the other guys started laughing and told me that he'd always wanted to meet a superhero. Everyone started laughing and the questions started. We spent a while talking about superhero stuff and then everything settled down. The consensus was that I would be the go-to person for moving. Lucky me! Nobody has better friends and family than me.

CHAPTER ELEVEN

A really cool thing happened the other day. I still hadn't made up my mind about whether or not to go public, so I was going for a run to help myself think. That's when I heard the strangest sound. I tried to figure out where it was coming from and determined that it was coming from the forest. There's lots of wildlife in the area- deer, wild turkeys and other birds, foxes, coyotes and even some bears - so I assumed that was what I heard.

As I got closer to the source of the sound,I saw it. It was a black bear and it was pacing around the base of a large tree. It saw me and I think I stopped breathing for a minute. I knew I could out run it, but I was hoping it wasn't in a fighting mood nonetheless.

I couldn't figure out what was wrong with the bear at first, but it was clearly in distress. It didn't look hurt, but it was fixated on the tree. I got as close as I could and that's when I saw what must be it's cub. Somehow, the little munchkin had gotten itself stuck in the roots of the tree. It was really wedged in there and was making the saddest sound I'd ever heard.

This was a unique problem! I knew I could get the cub out, but how did I get the mom to understand that I was trying to help? I started talking to her in a low, quiet voice. I told her my whole story from my diagnosis to the decision I was trying to make. As I was talking, both the mom and cub started to calm down. Mom stopped pacing and panting and the cub stopped crying. While I was talking, I moved slowly towards the cub until I was standing right next to it. Mom was watching me very closely, but so far she seemed to trust me.

I slowly started to bend down towards the cub. This was the time when I was really vulnerable to an attack from mama bear. I was down on my knees to get in a position where I could grab the roots and free the cub. Mom was starting to get agitated, so I had to move fast. I grabbed the root, pulled it up and freed the cub from the root bundle. The cub shook itself off and waddled over to it's mom. She sniffed the cub all over and it seemed like everyone was okay. That's when I noticed mom looking at me. What was she going to do? I gave her a wide berth so that she wouldn't feel trapped, but she didn't move. Was the cub hurt?

That's when the oddest, but most amazing thing happened. Mom started walking towards me. I had an initial reaction of panic, but I quickly realised that she wasn't charging me and didn't seem at all aggressive . I stood very still as she and the cub approached me. She stopped right in front of me and sniffed me. Then she leaned against me and I put my hand on her head. She sat down and looked right at me as if to say thank you. Then she and the cub walked off into the woods.

I think I stood there for at least ten minutes with a ridiculous grin on my face. If I never did anything else with my abilities, I would be okay with that after what had just happened. I ran home and told whoever would listen about the bears. My kids were so jealous!

Despite the high of saving the cub, I still had a decision to make. I'd put it off long enough. Well here goes nothing!

CHAPTER TWELVE

I've decided to go public. The only problem is that I have no idea how to do that. I could put a video on YouTube, but most people would think it's fake. I could go to the local newspaper or tv station, but they'd just think I'm nuts. This just doesn't seem to get any easier.

The best idea I could come up with involved another relative, my husband's cousin. She is on the local tv morning show and if I could talk to her, maybe she could get me some air time.

I contacted her and waited for her response. After a few days, she replied to say she was interested and we arranged to meet.

When we met at the coffee shop, she said she was intrigued by my message. I told her to keep an open mind and launched into my tale. I watched her face as I was explaining things and I could tell she was having a hard time believing me. Showing her my strength in public wasn't my plan, so I suggested that we finish our drinks and go outside where I would show her what I can do. She smiled and I could tell she thought that I was pulling her leg.

"So, I know this all sounds crazy. How can I prove this to you?" I asked.

She thought about it for a few minutes, looking around trying to find a fitting challenge.

She was looking towards a park and I saw a large boulder that I was pretty sure was the object she was focusing on. Good choice.

"If you can move that boulder, even a little bit, I'll believe you," she said.

We made our way over to the park. The boulder was almost as tall as me and several feet across. She gave it a push to make sure it was a real boulder. It didn't move. I've never tried to move anything like that, so I had no idea how much force it would take.

I took a deep breath, planted my feet and pushed as hard as I could. Apparently, I'm even stronger than I thought. I moved the boulder, but not just a couple of centimetres I rolled it over! That was a bit of a mistake, as it had been put there as a centrepiece. It actually rolled into a small tree and knocked it over. I looked over and shrugged my shoulders. My cousin looked shocked. I was looking at the boulder trying to figure out how to put it back, when we were approached by a police officer.

She looked at us. She looked at the boulder and broken tree. She looked back at us and asked if we knew what had happened.

Apparently it would cost somewhere in the range of $10 000 to put the boulder back in place and plant a new tree. She wasn't sure how we managed to dislodge the boulder, but she saw me leaning into it when it rolled. I told her I could fix the boulder, but I couldn't do anything about the tree. I promised I would pay for a new one.

Before anyone could say anything, I moved to the other side of the boulder and managed to push it back into place. By this time, a small crowd had gathered. Maybe going public would be easier than I thought. Almost all of them had phones and were busy taking pictures and posting them to various social media platforms. The officer had no idea what to do and reverted to crowd control.

At this point, the cat was out of the bag and my husband's cousin was looking at me with a smile - she wanted me on her show the next day. I was not prepared for the circus my life was about to become.

When I showed up at the tv station the next day, the public had already had 24 hours to watch the video of me moving a boulder over and over again. There was a large crowd of people gathered around the tv station. There were people with signs saying things like "we love superheroes", "save us", and "we love you". Then there were the signs that said things like "go back to your own planet", "you're a demon", and "abomination". The people at the station snuck me in the back door and soon after, I was live on the air.

We chatted a bit about my situation and then there was a segment where I was given a bunch of questions people had sent in. No, I'm not an alien and I don't know Superman - as far as I know, there are no other people like me. No, I can't fly. I can jump pretty high, but I haven't quite figured out landings yet - they hurt, so I'm still working on that. Yes, I am really strong, but I'm pretty sure I wouldn't be able to stop a car. I think that would really hurt. No, I'm not an Amazonian - as far as I know, they don't actually exist. No, I'm not an escaped government experiment. No, I wasn't born this way. No, I haven't met any super villains - again, I don't think there are other people like me. No, I don't have a costume, or a secret lair, or a sidekick. This is not a comic book or a movie. This is real life and what happened to me was a fluke. There's no conspiracy or whatever crazy stories people can come up with.

People also wanted to know what I'd do now that they knew who I was. Many of them wanted me to start patrolling the streets and take the law into my own hands.

"I'll will say this again - this is not a comic book or a movie! I already have a life. I have a family that I love. I already have a job that I really enjoy and I have no desire to roam the streets at night looking for people to beat up. I won't ignore situations that I encounter, but I am certainly not going to go out of my way to look for trouble."

I ignored a bunch of not-so-nice questions that came in on social media. Some I even reported to police.

Speaking of the police, I spent some time with them trying to convince them that I wasn't going to become a vigilante, taking out criminals as I saw fit. I told them the same thing I told my "fans", I wasn't going to look for trouble, but I wouldn't back away from it if faced with it. There was really nothing they could do, so I thanked them for their hospitality and went home. That was easy!

CHAPTER THIRTEEN

I'm not really sure what my life is like now. It moves between everyday, routine stuff like work and chauffeuring the kids around town, to crazy stuff like, well, like this.

I arrived at work one day to find a group of people waiting for me in the parking lot. I texted my coworkers to let them know that these people were trespassing and was assured that the police had already been called. The people in the group were carrying the same old nasty signs and chanting the same old nasty slogans about me. I stood there waiting for the police to arrive when one of the men approached me. I watched him carefully, checking to see if he had anything that could be used as a weapon.

They obviously forgot that I had enhanced hearing, but I heard someone else trying to sneak up behind me. I ducked at the last second as the other man took a swing at me with a crowbar. He stumbled and looked surprised. Two more men emerged from the group also carrying crowbars. This really wasn't fair. It wasn't like I had much formal fighting training, so this was going to be interesting to say the least.

There were at least twelve people in the group and if they all decided to attack at once, I'd have to make a run for it. The man who had missed took another swing and I managed to duck out of the way and grab the crowbar out of his hands. I threw it into the nearby field. So far, I hadn't said anything as I had discovered that trying to reason with people like this usually had the opposite effect. This time however, I yelled at the group to back off. I might as well have saved my breath.

Two more men in the group decided that this was their cue to attack. They were swinging their crowbars like swords and moved much quicker than I had given them credit for. I dodged the first swing, but the second one caught me on my left arm between my shoulder and elbow. I can only imagine the damage it would have done before I changed. Nonetheless, it hurt more than I care to admit and to make matters worse, the blow caused the crowd to cheer. This was getting out of hand and honestly, I was starting to get a little scared. I thought I could hear sirens, so I decided that it was now or never. I took a deep breath and charged at both men at the same time. Before they knew what had happened, I had disarmed them and knocked them to the ground.

Now I had the crowbars. The crowd was starting to move in and I really didn't want to hurt anyone - that would just prove them right - so I waited until they got a little bit closer and jumped over them. That's when the police pulled into the parking lot. Thanks for showing up.

The crowd started to run for their cars but were blocked in by the police. It was general mayhem for a few minutes as more police arrived and gathered up the "protesters" and their signs. I had already turned over the crowbars. They questioned me and asked if I needed medical attention. I pointed to the medical building and told them I had all the attention I needed inside.

When I got inside, one of the doctors took me into an exam room to take a look at my arm. It was already starting to feel better, so I told her not to worry. She took a look anyway, just to make sure.

I left the exam room and went straight to my manager's office. It was obvious what I had to do next. I went in, sat down and told her I was resigning. I would send her the official, written resignation the next day. She tried to convince me to stay, but we both knew that incidents like this would continue to happen. That could put the lives of patients and staff in danger and I couldn't be responsible for that. I said my goodbyes and wished them well. There was not much else for me to do. This was not a banner day for me - I loved that job.

I guess I'll have more time to do other things now like puzzles, reading, relearning the piano, teaching myself the guitar, riding my horse and practicing my jumping!

CHAPTER FOURTEEN

I had almost forgotten about the Think Tank that my sister had promised to consult with. She contacted me a few days ago to report their results. The report was quite long, so she gave me the condensed version over the phone and promised to send the full report later. I'm not sure I'll actually read it to be honest. On the other hand, I should have lots of time since I'm not working anymore.

The scenario she had given them was "is it possible for gene therapy to cause mutations in a person's DNA that would cause that person to develop enhanced abilities such as increased strength?". Seems simple enough.

Apparently, the report was 200 pages long! Being my sister, she had read the whole thing. They loved the question and had come to the conclusion that however fascinating the possibility of a human developing abilities is, it just isn't scientifically likely. The only plausible explanation they could come up with was that some kind of electrical charge could alter a person's cells. Maybe just enough to cause a change in a person's DNA?

Electrical charge? I thought back to what I assumed was a drug-induced hallucination during the procedure. Flickering lights and a feeling of static electricity - could that have really happened? Could that be what caused all this?

I guess we'll never know for sure.

I used to have a quiet, almost boring life - I actually enjoyed it. Now, I am recognized everywhere I go. I'm a strange kind of celebrity and no one really knows how to talk to me anymore. Some people (my family and friends) treat me the way they did before. Other people ignore me and still others are afraid of me. Then there's the small percentage of people who actively hate me. I'm not sure what they want me to do. It's not like I asked for this. My hope is that once people get over the initial shock of my existence, they'll go back to their own lives and leave my family and me alone. How long that will take is anyone's guess.

While waiting for people to get over themselves, I had some interesting things happen. The first was being invited to meet the Prime Minister of Canada . I was honoured and immediately responded yes. The next week, my family and I were sitting down with the Prime Minister and his family. He was very respectful and both he and his wife admitted that they wished they had abilities. Cool!

The very best thing that happened though was getting to meet Michael J Fox. Everyone with Parkinson's knows who he is and knows about his charitable organization. I had no idea that I was going to see him. He had contacted my husband and arranged to surprise me. I was just sitting at home doing a puzzle when the doorbell rang. No one else jumped up to see who it was, so off I went.

I opened the door and stood there in shock. Michael J Fox was standing on my front porch! Our dog looked at me and barked once as if to say "Invite him in". I regained some of my senses and said hello. My family and I spent the next three hours talking and laughing with Mr. Fox. It was one of the best experiences of my life. I guess developing abilities had some benefits that I hadn't thought of.

Over the next few months I got to meet more celebrities and politicians. I was also asked to give some talks at universities and conferences. I had settled into my new normal. I'm sure that there will be challenges and I will have to use my abilities now and then, but it's good to know that my world hasn't fallen apart. I have a lot of life left to live and I plan on making the most of it.

ABOUT THE AUTHOR

Dianne Bramble is a first-time author. She grew up in Kitchener, Ontario, with her parents, sister and large extended family. Dianne moved to Ottawa, Ontario with her future husband in 1992. Shortly after her wedding in 1996, Dianne decided to go back to university to become a registered nurse.

In September 2013, Dianne was diagnosed with early-onset Parkinson's disease following years of unexplained fatigue and motor-control issues. Determined to not let Parkinson's control her life, she immediately became active both for her own health and as an advocate for those with Parkinson's. Dianne attends horse riding lessons, works out with her personal trainer, Kate Spack (https://www.katespack.com) and participates in boxing training each week with Boxing4Health (https://www.boxing4health.com).   She is also an avid fundraiser for Parkinson's research and has attended the Parkinson's Superwalk in Ottawa every year since 2014.

Dianne lives in Carp, Ontario with her husband of 22 years, teenage daughter and teenage son. She is a long-time fan of superhero stories and has recurring fantasies of becoming one. She hasn't realized what is obvious to her friends and family: she already is a superhero!